MW00744862

AN ABSURD PALATE

An Absurd Palate

Alysa Levi-D'Ancona

QUERENCIA

Querencia Press, LLC
Chicago Illinois

QUERENCIA PRESS

© Copyright 2023
Alysa Levi-D'Ancona

All Rights Reserved

No reproduction, copy or transmission of this publication may be made
without written permission.

No paragraph of this publication may be reproduced, copied or
transmitted save with the written permission of the author.

Any person who commits any unauthorized act in relation to this
publication may be liable to criminal prosecution and civil claims for
damages.

ISBN 978 1 959118 31 2

www.querenciapress.com

First Published in 2023

Querencia Press, LLC
Chicago IL

Printed & Bound in the United States of America

For Wahaj,
        who savors each bite,
        who leans into the absurdities,
        who pushes me to keep writing,
        who helps me fall in
love   with life a little more

every day.

Il Menù

Aperitivo - 12
Spiced Wine

Antipasto - 13
Polka-Dotted Siren

Il Primo - 14
The Fin of A Bird

Il Secondo - 34
Like Water to Oil

Contorno - 47
molasses traps

Insalata - 48
Palate Cleanser

~~Aperitivo~~ Spiced Wine

Tines slice rhymes like spiced wine glistens lo. Oh, to know the low blow before it grows. A mister glissades and glisters on many blisters, lists messan on the chaise, lazing in tow like Rah making love to Elektra—sade heinie amazed in a maze. A blaze lit, a glaze split in the lagged zag of afterglow. She shines in sin and whines "mine in time," what a din sublime!

Antipasto
Polka-Dotted Siren

She's a polka-dotted dress: siren in enveloped dreams, lapping urgently like the crashing waves. Bells, sand crunching under hot rubber with the carmine chicharones and frozen popsicles.

Polka-dotted siren, slip on, slip into promised allure, dribble with splintered aftertaste. I slurp tentative sprinkles: buoyant chew of perfumed sand and polyester. Quick! Before she claims the melted bits!

Taunting sun on peekaboo no-thigh gap. Polka-dotted siren can't mask tufted expanse. Spaghetti-straps on a hanger fit better than on my baby fat shoulders. Numb ribbing roof of my mouth, phantom scales: embrace of almost ready, almost-promise fulfilled. She's never escaping the closet.

Battle tongues stronger than time's claim on messy reprieve. Warm skin, polka-dotted siren pulse slowing, shed my enveloped dreams, sink into home, umbrella nap until she radiates horizon.

Il Primo
The Fin of A Bird

Jamila watches from behind the bar as crimson treetops sway outside. Each swing of the door welcomes crisp October breeze.

It seems that work holds the years hostage, though it is more likely that working in a coffee shop called He-Brews It! in Manhattan is paltry to her. A crackling fireplace near the leather couch, bougie drink menus, and charcuterie boards: all were additions made by the new management to appeal to upper crust suckers. Jamila rolled her eyes at the improvements. Her new boss, Bacon, introduced the updates.

Jamila finds Bacon's name to be seemingly himself, though more in his upturned nose than pithy reference. The bored son of a rich New Yorker is nothing but a doll who gets to choose his playhouse. It's all make believe for a goateed baby like Bacon. When he changed the uniforms so Jamila resembled a red-clad bellhop, though...*that* was where she drew the line with his twisted aesthetic.

Today, a young med student fans her neck as the windows of He-Brews It! fog from body heat and the fireplace. Jamila doesn't know the woman's name but affectionately calls her Scarlet, because she often wears red nail polish that stands out in a sea of blue hospital scrubs. Scarlet hunkers down to study fat textbooks on Tuesdays and Saturdays—from the hellish hours of 5 a.m. until the normal morning rush begins.

Scarlet lifts up her kinky curls to relieve the sweaty stickiness blanketing her neck, unveiling sharp collar bones and a pendant necklace. *Good*, Jamila thinks, *Scarlet loves it.*

Jamila knows it's a stethoscope charm around Scarlet's neck, though she cannot technically see it from behind the bar. The barista smiles privately as the med student traces the pendant between her thumb and forefinger. Jamila thinks, *I've got a feeling that today will be a good one.*

Bacon would probably be irritated if he knew that Jamila refills Scarlet's cup every hour for free, but the young med student stood up for her one day when a particularly irritable doctor dumped his coffee all over the cash register. He complained that it didn't take a fucking neurosurgeon to make a half-decent cup of joe. And he ordered a powdered donut, *not* a peanut butter one, which would've landed him in the hospital. When Jamila apologetically handed him the correct donut, he bit into it once before throwing it at her face, leaving her in a cloud of sugary dust. Scarlet left Jamila a one-hundred-dollar bill after she chewed out the man. Though Jamila protested through reluctant tears, Scarlet insisted.

The same man sits at the table closest to the register today, with a salt-and-pepper beard, smug smile, and cheetah print polo.

Though Jamila hasn't seen him in here for three years at least, she has not forgotten the name she gave him after he webbed coffee all over her cash register: Homer. Like the yellow man-baby on television.

Scarlet bites her lips while fingering her materials. She taps her emptying mug against the laminate table, points at a diagram on the page of her book, snaps lead further down the mechanical pencil shaft, and scrolls through her Macbook screen. It is as if she is declaring, "I am a woman of science!" in her concentration alone.

Jamila wonders if the med student even knows how to turn the volume down in her cheeks as she studies, but that is what makes Scarlet so intrinsically her. She has a purity to her, the softest smile.

Homer, however, leers at Scarlet as though he's surveying her dancing half-naked on a pole. The look sends shivers down Jamila's spine.

The med student must not recognize the lewd gaze of her voyeur. *Sharks have the sea,* Jamila thinks to herself, *and yet this one chooses He-Brews It! for the hunt.*

The barista fantasizes what karmic divinity would tumble out of Scarlet's mouth if Homer deigned to speak to her. After the renewed annihilation of his character, what medication yard would he have to drag himself across?

It would be a shark revolution, a war against god-complexes.

Jamila's thought is interrupted when loud voices bring more crisp autumn air inside.

Screaming children in jerseys, one of them crumbling in tears, follow behind a chaperone ordering seven charcuterie boards. Jamila doesn't have the empathy to warn the adult that six thinly cut slices of gouda, seven grapes, and two walnuts on each platter will not sate the team's monstrous energy. So, she runs the transaction and hands the measly cheese platters to the deflated chaperone, who sighs at one child eating cheese under the cloak of the adult's skirt. Jamila notes silently that some people's children, clearly, have not been born enough to be in public.

The clown car of children has distracted Jamila for long enough; when she looks over at Scarlet's table, the textbooks are splayed out in vulnerable abandonment. Their owner has reappeared, instead, in the lap of Homer, who gives a bearded kiss to the back of Scarlet's head.

"You really should at least eat something," Homer chastises Scarlet. But his hand rests on her knee with the love of a mayor for his taxpayers. "A snack, at least."

"Coffee *can* be a snack," Scarlet protests.

"The food pyramid would beg to differ." He squeezes her thigh, then says, "Why don't you grab your stuff, bring it over here?"

Scarlet fans her hands dismissively. "It'll be fine over there for a few minutes."

"This isn't Gettysburg," he says.

"Stroudsburg," she corrects.

Even Jamila knows where Scarlet is from, she thinks.

"Regardless," Homer maintains, "this city will eat you alive if you're not careful."

Jamila takes some orders from a few more customers. She notices a palpable sorrow through Scarlet's motions as she transfers her study materials over to Homer's table and sits next to him. To the untrained eye, the two of them might look like an ideal pair: he in his white coat and she in her scrubs. But Jamila knows the dark underbelly of him, knows that the most precious songbirds can be captured into servitude.

A woman with bug-eyed sunglasses on the top of her head gnarls her words into whiny coils as she debates her order with her friend. Jamila doesn't bother naming the customer anything remotely name-like; Mantis will do, she thinks.

Barely visible beyond the two customers, Jamila's stomach drops when Scarlet caresses Homer's beard with painted nails. Jamila normally finds much temptation in Scarlet's kindness. But Scarlet's behavior now is spiraling. A distortion of the woman who once stood up to the monster she fondles now.

"Should I get the turmeric latte?" Mantis asks.

Mantis's friend sucks air through her teeth. "Turmeric doesn't taste good as a drink."

"Is there black pepper in it?"

"No," Jamila says.

As she stares at flashes of Homer past the two Upper East Siders, she realizes he looks a little older than the last time she saw him: his salt and pepper beard used to have more pepper in it. Now, there was more salt—tablespoons more.

Maybe that is where Scarlet's confusion lies, she thinks. *Not in character, but in converting teaspoons to tablespoons.*

Mantis puzzles at the menu. "Oh, hmmm."

"You know," Mantis's friend starts, "I heard that Gwyneth Paltrow drinks raw garlic lattes as of late."

Jamila watches Homer gesticulate grandiosely. She swears she hears him say: "A hose is very long. Not a lot of girth."

Mantis scoffs. "She does not."

"Does too."

Jamila's staring at Scarlet's mouth, waiting for words of disgust. Instead, she interprets Scarlet saying: "Are you talking about the Blue Man Group song?"

Maybe Jamila's lip-reading skills are not as sharp as she thought.

"Hey. Hey! Jam-uh-lah!" Mantis's friend butchers the letters on the barista's silver name tag. "Do you have those garlic lattes on your menu?"

Jamila prickles her nose. "No."

"On your seeeecret menu?" Mantis prods.

"We don't have a secret menu."

Mantis puckers her lips and raises her brow, "Starbucks has a secret menu."

"It's okay," Mantis's friend says. "Raw garlic is spicy anyway."

They order caramel macchiatos, walk out of Jamila's line of sight, and take their noisy chattering with them.

Their absence finally exposes Homer fondling the stethoscope charm that has found a home in the valley between Scarlet's prominent collar bones. Jamila seethes at the possession of what isn't his to have.

"You like how it looks on me?" Scarlet asks Homer.

"Uh, yeah!" He fumbles for enthusiasm as though it's difficult to locate, Jamila notes. "Yeah, I dig it."

"Well, don't act so surprised." Scarlet bites her lip like a shy child. "I mean, I know, I figured you snuck it in my textbook when I fell asleep at your place last night."

In Jamila's gut, a pit grows heavy in panicked gravity. Her heart races as she prays Homer will correct Scarlet's naïve mistake.

The doctor chews on the inside of his cheek.

Instead, he says, "Can't get anything past you, can I?"

Jamila's stomach boils.

An intrusive thought flutters into existence. She dismisses it, realizing the idea is scary, bad, and very un-Scarlet-like. She recalls that sometimes, you must go with your gut, but usually you shouldn't.

Homer snaps out of contemplation and settles into familiarity. "'Fell asleep'? Is that what we're calling it now?" His arm shifts, and Jamila realizes that he has buried his hand in Scarlet's lap.

The med student chuckles and brushes his arm away, much to Jamila's relief, "You know what I mean."

"I do." He kisses her cheek. "Only the best for the future doctor."

It was Pablo Neruda who said that forgetting is so short, but love is so long. At least, that's what Jamila thinks he said. It's been a while since she read his poetry, but she knows he knew his stuff. It must be this short forgetting that has caused the songbird to ensnare herself in the shark's cage.

No, that's unfair, Jamila scolds herself. It's not the songbird's fault for assuming the world is pure. It is the shark's fault for taking advantage of the feathered creature's trust. After all, a wing is the fin of a bird, if you think about it. Perhaps Scarlet looks at Homer and sees two birds of a feather.

Jamila looks over at their table once more and watches Homer bring Scarlet's hand to his lips. His eyes linger on her neck, where the pendant sparkles against her skin.

Then again, sometimes you *do* go with your gut.

Jamila leaves behind a customer mid-order. Smirking, she mixes an additive into a coffee pitcher and shuffles to save Scarlet from the trap.

Jamila becomes suddenly aware of her body as it moves away from the counter, though. Her mother used to say that she waddles side to side, her torso rigid like a penguin. Her mother isn't a problem anymore, just like Homer won't be soon enough. But her words still linger in Jamila's head. Maybe it is this inconveniently-timed recollection, or maybe it's her nearing Homer's table, but she becomes meek in her resolve.

As she stands above the couple, Jamila takes in the largeness of Homer. He is a formidable opponent, the size of Scarlet and Jamila together plus a few vertical inches. Jamila clenches her free fist and decides that she will rid Scarlet of sharks one at a time. Starting with the one filling the chair nearest the register—*her* register—that he once cobwebbed with coffee.

She runs through a slew of expletives in her head, thinking indirectly how lovely it would be for her fist to discover the caverns in his cheek.

When Homer raises his gaze to question her presence, Jamila's stare drops to the empty mug in front of her.

"Refill?" she forces through a clenched smile.

Scarlet turns, and the world stops as the women lock eyes: as though all the gestalt switches have activated to reveal the larger meaning of Jamila's three years of small gestures.

The med student smiles, and while Jamila wondered moments ago if she maybe made Scarlet up, Jamila's chest softens as she tops off Scarlet's mug with the nutty coffee.

"That necklace," Jamila breathes, focused on Scarlet. "It's so beautiful."

Feeling for the pendant, Scarlet reaches for Homer's hand and grins warmly at him. "Thank you," she says.

"I, um, I am thinking about buying one for my, uh, sister," Jamila says, turning to Homer. "Where, where did you buy it, if I may ask?"

Homer's breath catches in his chest before he lets out an exhale. "Oh, uh, you know, I'm not sure I remember. Not a jewelry guy, normally, you know." He winks at Scarlet.

Jamila leans into her words with growing ease: "Hmm, I could swear I've seen it somewhere..."

"Sorry, can't be more help."

Scarlet sips coffee while rubbing Homer's palm meditatively with her thumb.

"*Actually,*" Jamila jumps at the thought, "I remember now! It was Sephora. Did you get it there?"

"Right!" Homer jumps at the name. "Sephora. Yes, the woman there was so helpful."

There is a lull hanging above the table. The women know it, but Homer doesn't. There's an uneasiness in Scarlet's demeanor now. She waits for Homer to continue. He doesn't. He relaxes into his chair.

"Are you sure it was Sephora, babe?" Scarlet chooses her words slowly. "With the black and white stripes?"

"Of course, sweetheart." His words cut across the table and a startled Scarlet withdraws her hand. "You think I don't remember the name of the place I spent two hours looking for a gift for you?"

Jamila smiles as Homer digs deeper into the lie.

"Noah," Scarlet murmurs. Her easy enthusiasm has vanished from her face; her gaze is heavy now. "Sephora doesn't sell jewelry."

Homer's jaw clenches, and he rolls it back and forth in silence.

Jamila lets the tension linger, relishing Homer's ignorant undoing, before she decides to interject.

"Oh. My mistake."

Scarlet's lips part with no words escaping them. Jamila seizes the moment to refill the coffee. She pours some in Homer's half-empty mug without asking.

It's Homer that breaks the silence.

"Don't you have something else to do?" he directs to the barista, placing a hand on Scarlet's thigh again. She brushes his hand off.

Jamila stares at him with a doe-like expression. "Sorry, sir, just doing my job."

His eyes narrow with a burning fury, but then the muscles under his salt and pepper beard start twitching.

"Wait. I know you—"

"Whoa-hoooo there!"

Jamila's skin crawls as the nasally voice of Bacon encroaches. He appears next to her, their hips an inch apart.

"Howdy there, folks! You're in good hands with Jamila here. My name is Bacon. Anything I can do to make your morning perkier?"

Jamila restrains the urge to groan, but as Homer's glare bores into her, she is suddenly grateful for Bacon's intervention.

"We're good," Homer snips. "Just enjoying some time with my lovely girlfriend."

The description sounds more a threat than a statement, but Bacon does not seem to notice.

"Ah, love. Love, love, lovely couple." Bacon puts his arm around Jamila's red, buttoned bellhop dress. "At He-Brews It! we *love* love!"

Scarlet points between Jamila and Bacon and asks, "Oh, so you two are—"

"Bacon and I *work* together," Jamila spits.

A shiver runs down her spine, and when she finds Scarlet's face again, Jamila is held hostage in what feels like years again, but this time, she doesn't mind. The med student's eyes—the most olive green—twinkle with a new emotion.

"So, the manager of He-Brews It! is Bacon?" Homer asks with condescension and inquiry.

Jamila is unsure if Scarlet can hear her heart racing, but she knows that the two of them are bound in an understanding. Scarlet mouths, *Thank you*, and Jamila wonders if the med student is aware just how much she will thank her soon.

"Unique, isn't it?" Bacon beams. He explains that he earned his name when he converted from playing guitar to bass. A bass-convert.

Maybe, if she screams it in her thoughts, Scarlet will hear it, *I think about you all the time. I think about you ALL THE TIME.*

"Bayyy connn! Get it?" he chortles.

"Ah," Homer murmurs. He sips his coffee at last.

Finally.

Jamila pretends the shark doesn't exist. She hovers over Scarlet now. Close enough to feel her body heat. Close enough to stare into those olive green eyes and see flecks of gold in them. She's never been close enough to see gold in them.

Scarlet's gaze is laser-focused on Jamila, who catches her breath at the intense connection.

"I bet you think about me," Jamila prays.

But, she says it out loud. Or maybe that is precisely how she wanted to say it.

Jamila feels all three of them staring at her as though she is staked with wooden poles. She feels disoriented in her body, as though it is wobbling slack.

And though she wishes Scarlet would respond, the object of her affection becomes glassy-eyed. She doesn't shove away Homer's hand when he reaches for her this time.

"Wowza," Bacon says. "C'mon Jam-Jam. That's enough of a break. Enjoy your day, lovebirds!"

He ushers her toward the entrance of the employee-only area. Before she has a chance to collect herself, she hears a man gagging, a loud thunk, then a squeal from Scarlet. Jamila would recognize her voice anywhere. The ruckus is followed by loud voices anew and a scream to call an ambulance.

Truly, what medication yard would save Homer now?

As Bacon rushes in a panic toward the collapsed doctor, Jamila smirks and empties the pitcher of coffee down the drain. Karmic divinity, indeed.

In the shark revolution, Homer forgot that gods take many forms, that this city will eat you alive if you're not careful.

"A wing *is* the fin of a bird," she mutters under her breath, "if you think about it."

She knew today would be a good one.

Il Secondo
Like Water to Oil

The dimpled woman retires into her being when her boots echo on stone floors. Wurch Hall was distinguished in its ability to make any expert of CXBS wonder at their smallness, to anonymize and familiarize. But unfamiliar fingers would find her soon.

She previewed the assessment before making the journey and, thus, feels ready. There's a tickling flutter of nerves, but she knows she will succeed with capable grace. The woman walks into The Boil, orders a dish for 15 PDs, and disappears into a booth in a corner.

Midtwen-parts pass before the man shuffles across stone, his steps less certain than that of the woman. She catches a glimpse of him under her curtain bangs but thinks better of waving him over. This is part of the belldrummer, she reminds herself. And so she waits.

Some midone-parts later, she sees his scuffed boots occupy the mosaic stone floor of her booth.

"Miss, Ms. Erghuo?" the man asks.

She faces him now—pointy nose, unevenly gray beard, plaid pocket square in tan dress shirt. Like water to her oil, Pedsben is everything she hoped he'd be.

"Hezly moved to Orsymo," she corrects. "I'm her replacement."

"And you are Miss...?"

It's always the men that insist on addressing women with a title, she notes internally. Her nose tickles; she resists scratching it. "I find the Ms. so impersonal. Zharani is just fine."

Remaining with one leg crossed over her knee—folded in her seat like a labyrinth—she offers no hand to shake.

This does not escape Pedsben, and he nods once before he lowers himself to sit across from her. He crosses one leg over his own knee, thinks better of it, and uncrosses them.

Pedsben puts his sticky hands on the table; he finally can see Zharani under the yellow light of the booth. He notes the curtain bangs that hide her forehead. She would be prettier without them, he thinks, but he knows he is lying to himself. For as Pedsben studies the woman in front of him, he finds a winsome puzzle. Though it's at least 1.1 UO inside the bustling Boil with not a cloud in the sky outside, she sits with a ruby, rubberized raincoat zipped nearly all the way up. And yet, it is open enough to see the shadowed hint of cleavage. She catches his wandering eye and he shuffles in his seat, crossing his legs anew.

Pedsben interrupts his poor manners, "I wish she would've told me is all."

Zharani presses her lips into a tight smile. "Yes, but as we always say, we catch the still stars—"

"—with chocolate arrows," he grumbles. He knows it's Zharani's duty to state the Name mantra, but he wonders at it, remembers the reason for the meeting in the first place, and shuffles again.

She twitches her flat nose, wishing she could scratch it. "Right, then. Hezly briefed me on your parans from last month."

"Great," he strains enthusiasm.

This cushioned seat is dreadful, he thinks. It squeaks as he fidgets, and he finds himself ankling her under the table. Pedsben freezes, but it is she who accidentally ankles him this time.

Zharani continues, "This month's only half-way through, but you've always been a top contributor. Just a few thousand more parans and you'll be close to winning the SNR promo!"

Here we are, ankling each other in a diner, Pedsben muses. A small voice reminds him to be firm with the business at hand until moseying is on the table, though he would fancy himself a mosey, he thinks.

"Listen, Miss Zharani—"

"Leave the missus at home, please," she says.

Pedsben hears her slowly. She must have seen my band, he thinks to himself, blushing. Improper, yet enticing. But business, yes. Business.

Zharani is well aware he thinks her ignorant. She sees him fidgeting with his ring, sees his beady pupils flickering to her lips every time they part.

He asks himself how she will react, chest thumping. Ms. Erghuo was always so patient. The woman before him is warmly plastic, violently scrupulous. A winsome puzzle, indeed.

Tiagin's playbook for management, rule #84 like water to oil, she thinks.

"Pedsben?" she says.

"Yes?"

"I am listening, as requested."

She places her elbows on the table and rests her dimpled chin in her palms, expectant. She waits for Arc's Taxonomy to take hold, is ready for his next words or lack thereof.

He knows that to be lost is to be ex-found, which is to say that Pedsben is struggling to place where he has left his resolve. Under the powdery stairs of manhood, perhaps, as his missus might argue. He thinks of his missus, of their changing bodies. Does a body exist if it is not touched? He will leave forty as a small, untouched man if he does not do what he set out to do today.

No, he tells himself, thinking of the exhausted names that he's harangued into this same dilemma, that won't return his calls or sell their parans anymore. Come to think of it, he is Zharani to his own Pedsbens, and as such it is his duty, no, his power to stand up to *his* Zharani.

"While I have been, just, grateful for this business opportunity," Pedsben begins, "I cannot—"

A waiter places the food in front of them, and Zharani mumbles thanks. Their eyes linger on the steaming mash of food. The more he studies it, the more it looks like the floor unpeeled if it ever were to.

"Please, help yourself," she offers.

Pedsben's insides twist until his stomach grumbles. When he swallows inward, her mouth curls devilishly.

She considered the rubric when she planned this meeting, which is why they are in Wurch's Boil and not elsewhere. Somysev's acoustics are far too efficient, as the multitude of conversations in it sounds Gregorian chant-esque. Bazol's could only be described as under-tiful, and, well, no self-respecting person calls a meeting in Sade Bistro. The Boil is perfect to take a man such as Pedsben and unhinge him. So many opportunities for meaningful releases and meaningless ones, too.

"Unless, that is," she says, "you'd rather I order you dundra cheese?" She peels her eyes open in earnest, searching for a waiter that will never make it back to the table before the trap is set.

It has been too many midtwo-parts since he ankled her, and now he worries he made the whole thing up.

Pedsben regrets the intervention and sputters apologies. "Oh, it's, um, no, no. I insist it's no trouble," he says, ex-found once more.

He digs for a saving grace, but as sweat accumulates in dribbles along his spine, he wonders if Zharani understands how his body Achilles falls to her metallic gaze every time she peeks out from those curtain bangs, how he cannot bear the notion that she considers him so closed-minded as to refuse a meal—

no matter how unpeeled-floor-like it is—for mere *dundra cheese*.

So he melts and says, "I, do...do I use a fork or spoon?"

She lets him scan the table for utensils another midfour-parts before she states, "Hands."

They look at each other for another midten-parts, maybe even midthir.

It's tantalizing, he thinks, how glimpses falling into another feel a lot like divided elongation.

Good, she thinks. We are in the zone of rebimal development.

With unencumbered gravity, his fingers find the mash and scoop them to his lips. Gritty, he notes at first, but it tastes like nothing he's ever known. Maybe it's the humdrum of The Boil's patrons—how can they chortle in their steeped brews and denim sequins? Or perhaps it's the half simplicity of Zharani's watching him as he licks the gritty food from his claimed ring finger. Did she just bite her lip? Is this what feeling himself savored might mean? He never considered himself a romantic, but with newfound levity, he dives into the mash again, using both hands to shovel the meal past his teeth.

Zharani leans back against the plasticky foam of the booth. She relishes in the trappings, he in unbound ease. It is not that she expects him to have any grasp of the situation. On the contrary, his reaction is normal, exactly why she factored in p±1 during the preliminary 6W evaluation. But as she thinks about all the wonders learned from this line of work, she reflects that men like Pedsben are precisely why she finds oblique inspiration—not in *them*—in herself. An out of body experience, in a way, to watch the predator as it lures the prey.

They are all the same, she reflects. All previous clients of hers are Pedsben and all future ones will be him too. It is the shaffoning of the situation that makes each encounter remarkable and yet un- at the same time. The backwards design is all the same. But the thrill from fluidity reminded, of feeling the present—not even sex could give her such a power high.

Zharani unfurls in her seat as she fingers a piece of clumsy lemongrass in the mash, guiding it to her lips as she holds it between her canines and tears off a bite. A glob of grey-brown mash tumbles from

Pedsben's mouth as she chews. She offers the lemongrass to him. He swallows the food already renting space on his tongue, then obliges, delicately placing the plant on the open real estate before closing his mouth. He traces the lemongrass to taste the essence of her, realizing an essence is not all he wants anymore.

I wake eternal, he thinks.

All the same, she thinks.

It is time, Zharani reminds herself. "Now, about the LTS," she says.

"Hmphh," Pedsben garbles past the saliva and food. He gulps it down, sweat finding itself on his mashy hands now as he fingers his glasses.

"Another seventy parans at 405 PDs," she suggests.

He clears his throat, wondering whether he should mention that he only sold thirty parans last month, that he has only 1000 PDs in his account, or that he didn't recruit enough last month as part of the jigwat approach. He considers the wavering sunlight as it hits Zharani's raincoat.

Pedsben allows himself to imagine her joyous rain creating hearts that know what their bodies already know. But when he lets his mind carry itself away, he thinks only of Zharani tucking him into bed.

The tingles in Zharani's nose pepper like numbness, she notes. She cannot wait to exit The Boil to scratch it. She bites her lip to stretch out the skin without touching her face.

"Make it eighty parans," he counters.

Her mouth twitches into that devilish smile and whispers, "That's my guy."

"Hey, can I ask a favor?"

"For you? Anything," she lies.

"Can you..." he trails off.

He swallows inward again.

"Listening, as requested," Zharani says.

"Can you, can you hold me?"

Zharani puckers her lips in thought, then pats her lap. The plasticky fabric creaks as she uncrosses her legs.

Pedsben raises himself to walk to the other side of the booth and sits, shuffling over to her. While feeling her body's warmth, he realizes he forgot what one's jutting toward another leads to.

Her itchy, wide nose prickles at the odor of his residual nervous sweat.

Backwards design, she reminds herself.

Her body a touch away, he thinks.

His body waxes the closer he gets, she thinks, and opens her arms to him.

As he positions his buttocks on her lap and leans against her frame, she cradles his damp back with one hand and strokes his graying beard with the other. Though he never verbalizes this desire, she starts humming the instrumental tune of the Name's mantra. He thinks of the smallness of womb feet and hands, and wishes, for a moment, to be as pro-rest as ex-found. In his own private breaking, sticky tears trickle down Pedsben's weathered cheek.

The waiter is all too kind some midtwen-parts later. He notices the depressing man in rattling snores still on Zharani's lap, offers to help put him to bed on the outside pavement. When they drop him to the concrete, Pedsben rips another deep snore.

"He's out like a kohlron," the waiter cracks.

Zharani chuckles. "It's no wonder. With a work ethic like his, he's only a few thousand parans away from an SNR promo."

The waiter raises his eyebrows. "Wow, an SNR promo," he sighs, thinking of the decades of waiting tables he'll have to do to put 20% down on one.

Her nose is begging to be scratched, but Zharani twitches the urge away, another opportunity ripe and unfolding before her. "How would you like the freedom of being your own boss?" Like water to oil, the dimpled woman thinks.

They're all the same.

They descend the wooden steps, leaving Pedsben to the street.

Contorno

molasses traps

She works in molasses   traps. time moves

parallel in Her   embrace—sweet   quicksand smothers

     disobedience. at   some   point, ensnarement

     is all you

     know. a hive-   mind, you mimic the

1 teaspoon of gaslight,
1 liter of looking anywhere but in,   and
3 cups of complisults.

you're trusted   with the Family   recipe now.

sticky, hardened   armor molten   into skin.   the world

won't know you   were boiled alive   if you

     come out sweet,   if you

     ensnare it

     before   it realizes

     you've followed

Her blueprint,

     before   you accept that

   you,   too,

     work in molasses   traps.

Insalata

Palate Cleanser

Xenor meanders across cool tiles, groaning as she ponders the poor mechanics of feet. With all that flat real estate across webbed skin, one wonders why there isn't hair covering absolutely *everywhere* below the ankle. Even the ursine lot have fur between the toes—and they swim! If fur is practical enough protection to swim with, then it damned well is practical enough protection against ceramic tiles in a $4000 a month apartment downtown.

She looks at herself, leaning on the granite countertop of her vanity. Will she want to go to DiscoReek or lay low at WormWilly tonight? Or, will Munther prowch up the courage to ask her out again? She runs her tongue along her gritty, slimy teeth—as though a snail left its prints across crumbled graham crackers.

As Xenor exhales hot, she realizes Munther will eventually wake to this image of her. If things keep going well, that is. One day, he will exit slumber to find Xenor in her ice-foot, snail-trail-mouth glory and think, "Yes. This is my person."

But that day is not today, so she grabs the tube from the sink and squid-squelches the inky line onto her brush. She observes the shiny mass, shoves it in her mouth, and starts scrubbing at her teeth.

A thought halts the motion. She removes the brush from her lips, crouches down, and begins scrubbing between her toes instead.

Formaggi e Frutta
Quiet's Clarity

In the quiet moments, the earth unfolds
its ribs. You hear the roaring focus of heart beating
hope into pulp: orange juice oozed
by the carefree hands of children.

That metronome slows its pulse—churning
taffy out of time—and with it, the flavor-
less chew of sinking into jellied sand.
These moments are stolen kisses
in the fog. Absconded clarity looks a lot

like addiction: the ache in your
tongue when it holds back
its virulent words; the tears'
willowing like capillaries' cobwebs
when loneliness rears
its ugly permanence; tastes metallic as though

an epistolary truth could ever
find poetry's melody in your pen-
chant for fearing
the quiet.

Dolce

Daphne

The book of us rolls into glass, tilled then kilned as shards starred become constellations—Apollo for Daphne, whose extremities salve inky cuts. Bay leaves sway in sun rays so we vow to stay in bed, charting where your constellations will be for other lovers to see, while I sink my roots into the flooring, wondering how immortal my laurels will be when they read the story of you and me.

Caffè

Blanketed Reincarnation

You finish with the beginning: blanketed reincarnation
between the forest of icy berries. Blushing horizon
entices suspended allure, a fullness
matched with the sharp comfort of frost on hot
cheeks. You lust after
the loudness of quiet, the fullness of consuming
pine's scent, the swallow's song, of being
pinned down by the mountain's
grandiosity. Snow-sheets bed
abbreviated death, yet you are not done
with the creamy bite, nor the fruit
of promises to come.

Digestivo

Poetics

Perspective starts with innocence—a desire to be a certain way and then a reckoning that reality doesn't align with an ideal. Then, when we become aware of just how deep the disconnect is, how easy it is to interpret multiple truths in a reading, we become disillusioned. We grow angry, lost, reliant on whoever promises grounding. We become aliens to ourselves as we question the very foundation of our understanding, not only of those around us, but ourselves. In a way, the person who is certain in their perspective is both the genius and the jester: they have found clarity in obscurity while ignoring subjectivity. Where do we fall on the scale of genius, and where does the storyteller's duty lie if not in subverting comfort in the absurdities of the truths we tell ourselves?

An Absurd Palate walks through the ten-course meal often served in Italian restaurants for dinner: *aperitivi, antipasti, primi, secondi, contorni, insalate, formaggi e frutta, dolci, caffè,* and *digestivi.*

There is a sacred art—though some may call it a science—to dining in Italian culture. You must eat in the order of which is most healthy for digestion. This dinner format is reserved for special gatherings, guests, and celebrations. Most Italians will only make themselves a *primo* or a *secondo* and *contorno* for dinner. Though, they rarely miss the opportunity for an evening *caffè*—good for the gut!

On a slightly oblique note, many of the works in this chapbook were created by lists of various types. I would gather random assortments of names, phrases, and dialogue before starting a piece, then I would use that list as a guide to weave into the story or poem, much like a puzzle that I had to work my way out of. To create stories out of fragments and make it look like they belonged together from the beginning is akin to cooking. All dishes are an amalgamation of ingredients. The ingredients for a cake, muffin, and cookies are nearly identical, and yet they all come out differently. Similarly, a pasta alla ragú is hardly dissimilar from a curry with roti, which is even more similar to a pizza. These dishes all tell different stories of culture and family, and yet, they are united in their ingredients and communal power.

The menu of *An Absurd Palate* begins with the *aperitivo*, which is when small snacks are laid out on the table and cocktails are served (though traditionally, Italians like to consume a lighter, dryer drink like spumante, wine, prosecco, or aperol spritz). The prose poem, "Spiced Wine," opens the collection with a surreal, smooth entrance into the chapbook. Many of the words are related to each other in sound and mouth feel, but the poem is light, airy, even tantalizing in its rhyme scheme. This poem was inspired by a prompt related to Harryette Mullen and *Sleeping with the Dictionary*, where I took the words derivative of the word glitter and gathered false cognates in a list. The story that came together was one of an evening at the ballet, followed by a romantic encounter with spiced wine. Just looking at the words provides the perspective of ease, as with an aperitivo, but upon another look, it's evident that there is a lamenting, even sorrowful undertone to the poem.

The *antipasto* is the appetizer of the meal, often served with *salumi* (cured meats) or regional specialties. Just like with an array of assorted meats, I collected lists of descriptions of foods, surroundings, textiles, and memories around them before beginning my weaving. As such, "Polka-Dotted Siren," inspired by the prose poetry of Khadijah Queen's *I'm So Fine*, narrates the story of a polka-dotted dress ("she") and a young girl ("I") as she aims to embody sensuality in a garment. When she realizes that her body is still too gangly, awkward, pubescent, and un-sexy, she shoves the dress back into the closet, never wearing it. At the end, she finds acceptance by putting away the dream of being something she is not ready for yet. While the story is about a dress, it is also about growing up and the perspectives we and society place on us. This prose poem serves as a taste for the main course, as it introduces the disarming perspective of personifying a dress and describing events in fragments.

Considered the second-heaviest part of the meal, the *primo* (the "first" course) is the pasta or risotto dish: the carbohydrate. Many Italians will only eat the *primo* if they are cooking for themselves at home; "The Fin of a Bird" occupies this spot in *An Absurd Palate*. I collected a list of overheard dialogue, lyrics, humor, language play, and shoving pages of books together to make unusual pairings, inspired by both Renee Gladman's *Houses of Ravicka* and Don Mee Choi's *Hardly War*. In the story, I unpack flawed perspectives through Jamila, a character who has created narratives and truths about people she witnesses in a coffee shop, namely Scarlet and Homer. While Jamila starts out as the sympathetic narrator who observes a world of "upper crust suckers," the reliability in her storytelling loses footing, and by the end, we are left wondering if Scarlet and Jamila have a connection, if Homer deserves his karma, and if Jamila is more shark than songbird. With absurd one-liners woven throughout, the tale begs readers to examine their own biases and question why they root for someone's downfall.

Undoubtedly the heaviest part of the meal, the *secondo* (or "second" course) is a meat dish, making "Like Water to Oil" an obvious fit. It not only is the densest of the stories, but it is the most absurd; most Italians opt to skip the *secondo* in order to save room for *il dolce*. Inspired by lists of places, misaligned book pages from Chanel Miller's *Know My Name*, and Renee Gladman's *Houses of Ravicka*, "Like Water to Oil" follows Zharani and Pedsben in equal narration, often juxtaposing their perspectives of the events in contradiction. While Pedsben fancies himself in the driver's seat of their business arrangement and in favor of Zharani's affection, Zharani finds him disgusting, saying only what she must in order to close the deal. With the made up language of the world they inhabit, the reader has little comfort in the story, thus aligning with the wide-eyed confusion of Pedsben at times. Similar to the *primo*, the reader both roots against Pedsben and for Zharani and yet pities Pedsben's fate.

The *contorno* (side dish) is rarely served except by more health-conscious Italians. *Contorni* often include roasted vegetables, like potatoes, carrots, tomatoes, or green beans. "molasses traps" fits the role of the side dish in *An Absurd Palate*, as it is a poem of caesuras (inspired by Krista Franklin's works in *Too Much Midnight*) telling the story of learning the family recipe: "ensnarement." While many families pass down recipes, this one of molasses traps "smothers disobedience," creating a cycle of abuse. Since familial emotional abuse is difficult to confront, often overlooked, and served with the heaviness of the *primo* and *secondo*, it best matches with the *contorno* as a reluctant perspective of absurd inheritance.

If the *contorno* is scarce at the dinner table, the *insalata* (or salad) is even scarcer. Channeling Renee Gladman's use of nonlinear storytelling, "Palate Cleanser" plays both on the transition from the first half of the meal to the next (there are still four more courses after this one!). After the dark nature of the previous short stories, Xenor's absurd pondering while brushing her teeth breaks the tension with a ridiculous, lighthearted perspective on the beginning of a budding relationship and cleanliness.

Fancier events serve a course of *formaggi e frutta* (cheese and fruit): usually local delicacies. At this point in the meal, most people are stuffed, so they start to question whether or not they should quit while they're ahead. But, you *cannot* deny a course—or really any food—from an Italian host! I wrote "Quiet's Clarity," when I was alone, anxious, and overthinking, which embodies this point in the meal. There are moments when I feel everything is clear, and then others where everything I have believed to be clear is a lie, calling into question my own perspective and analysis of reality. The poem "unfolds" on an existential level, questioning what truly can be defined as clarity, truth, belonging, loneliness, even art. I was inspired by Emily Mundy's tension in her line breaks, focusing specifically on the exigence of anxiety.

The *dolce* (sweet or dessert) is the last food course. Channeling the prose poetry of Harryette Mullen once again, "Daphne" recounts the Greek myth of Apollo and Daphne—where the river nymph turned into a laurel tree to escape the aggressive love of Apollo—from Daphne's perspective. At first glance, the poem reads as a love story of equals; after all, both are immortal and healers. Yet, there is an imbalance between the two: Apollo is immortalized in the heavens and painted positively, whereas Daphne's laurels have been appropriated by Apollo as symbols of art and poetry. She is grounded in place, never to join the heavens like her stalker. It is a story of tainted love and victory, falsely sweet.

Using one of CAConrad's prompts, I pulled phrases from my surroundings, ate berries, and listened to music while crafting "Blanketed Reincarnation" for the *caffè* (coffee). Italians end their large meal with a shot of espresso—*never* with milk—to jumpstart digestion and stave off the food coma. The poem explores the unsettling beauty and comfort you find on a quiet mountain in the winter: a feeling of belonging, smallness, and awe at the "grandiosity" of nature. There is both death and rebirth in the winter forest, a danger of losing oneself and finding oneself: where "you finish with the beginning." Yet, the perspective also hints at a visceral, lustful encounter, playing on the absurdity of bedding a mountain.

All Italian meals end with the *digestivo* (digestive), which is served with a hard liquor that accelerates the digestion process such as limoncello or grappa. In *An Absurd Palate*, it only makes sense that the poetics aid in the digestion of the courses that precede it.

Most importantly, dining together is a journey in and of itself. To eat together is to swap stories between those you spend time with: some lyrical, some anecdotal, and some fictional. The dinner table is both where people can drag out tensions of the world beyond them or where they can choose to leave behind reality. Many families, mine included, have irreconcilable differences, but at dinner they must come together and find their similarities. In a way, *cena*, or dinner, exists on an alternate timeline, one where perspectives meld together and reality falls away. Thus, what better medium to digest the absurdities of perspective than a fixed dinner menu?

Acknowledgments

"Blanketed Reincarnation" was published in *The RavensPerch* on February 22, 2022.

"Daphne" was published in *Clamor's* 2022 issue. *Clamor* is a literary journal by University of Washington Bothell.

"Palate Cleanser" was published in *Stone Pacific Zine's 9*th issue on December 22, 2022.

"molasses traps" was published in *Occulum's* 13th issue on November 5, 2022.

"The Fin of a Bird" was published with *Caustic Frolic* in their Spring 2023 issue.

"Like Water to Oil" was published with *Cream Scene Carnival Magazine* in their Mayday issue in 2023.

CPSIA information can be obtained
at www.ICGtesting.com
Printed in the USA
BVHW050510200623
666137BV00003B/78